The Elephant Quilt

Stitch by Stitch to California!

HO FOR CALIFORNIA!

Utah Territory

Colorado River

California

New Mexico Territory

Los Angeles

Gila River

Gila Trail

Apache Pass

Mexico

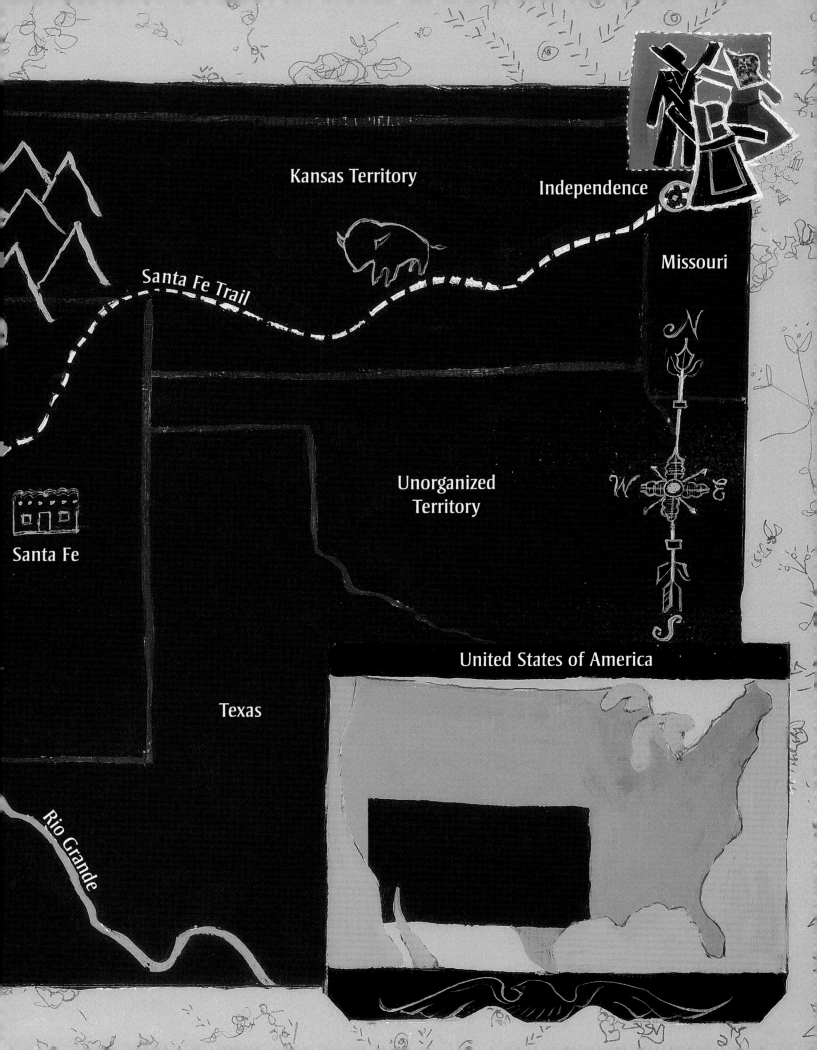

THE

ELEPHANT QUILT

Stitch by Stitch to California!

Susan Lowell   Pictures by Stacey Dressen-McQueen

MELANIE KROUPA BOOKS • FARRAR, STRAUS AND GIROUX

NEW YORK

Slow, slow, slow go the wagon wheels.

But my little needle flies quickety, quickety, quick.

We're going to California in a wagon train, Mama and Papa and Grandma and my big brother, Lorenzo, and me, Lily Rose. I'm *sewing* to California!

"Tiny stitches, Lily Rose," says Grandma. "Tiny stitches make big strong quilts." She pulls a scrap of ruby-red silk out of her bag.

"Ooh!" I say. "Let's sew *red* in our quilt, Grandma! Let's make fire and roses!"

"We'll see," says Grandma.

Inside our new blue wagon we've got a kettle and a cooking pot, a barrel of crackers, a hammer and nails, some blankets and bonnets and buckets and books, Mama's flower seeds, and Grandma's scrap bag, just jam-packed with the pieces of our quilt.

The day we left home, Grandma embroidered on the first piece of the quilt: "Missouri, April 15, 1859." And then she stitched three words more on another piece: "Ho for California!"

"We're going to see the Elephant," says Lorenzo.

That's what people say when they head west.

"What *is* the Elephant?" I ask.

"Don't you wish you knew?" he teases.

Oh, it's something mighty big, I reckon. Something powerful strange. Like a real live elephant, but even bigger—stranger—wilder—scarier! Something BO-dacious!

As he walks along, Lorenzo likes to sing:

"Ho for California!
The only place for me..."

Why are we going West? Oh, we have lots of reasons! "For gold!" says Lorenzo. "For land," says Papa. "For health," says Grandma.

Mama doesn't really want to go. But she doesn't want to stay behind, either.

And me? *I* want to see the Elephant, *whatever* it may be!

Slow, slow, slow we roll along. Stitch, stitch, stitch, and Kansas goes on nearly forever, until one day . . . Oh, mercy me!

"Looky there!" cries Lorenzo.

"Golly, what a whopper!" I shout. *"It's the Elephant!"*

"No, Lily Rose," says Papa quickly. "It's a buffalo bull. Stand back!"

So I do.

Sitting by the campfire, night after night, Papa traces a line on the map.
That's our road, the Santa Fe Trail. By and by, tall mountains rise up before us.

"Giant fingers chopped 'em out of purple cloth and hemmed 'em up against
the sky," I think, as I sit sewing. And the tip-tops of those mountains are pure
shining white, the splendidest sight I ever saw.

"Oh me, oh my," Mama frets, "I hope we don't have to climb them."

"Can we sew mountains in our quilt, Grandma?" I ask. "And sky?"

"Well," says Grandma, smiling, "there's a quilt pattern called Delectable
Mountains. It's real pretty. So's Sunburst. And I like Barn Raising, Princess
Feather, Wild Goose Chase, Blazing Star, Wandering Foot . . ."

"I believe your papa slept under *that* one," says Mama with a sigh.

"But what's the name of *our* quilt?" I wonder.

"We'll see," says Grandma.

On Independence Day we camp at the foot of the mountains, and Lorenzo vanishes.

"Rattlesnakes, earthquakes, panthers . . ." Mama worries. "Blizzards, lizards, bandits, kidnappers, forest fires, deep dark pits, cannibals, grizzly bears . . ."

"Elephants?" I say to myself.

But at that very moment Lorenzo waltzes into camp.

"Open your mouth and shut your eyes!" he hollers.

"EEK!" My mouth is full of mountain snow. Snow on the Fourth of July!

At long last, we roll into Santa Fe, where Mama buys beans and flour, Grandma picks out pins and thread, Papa gets a new map, and Lorenzo meets a miner. In his scruffy hand a fat nugget glows like a hot coal.

"Slathers of gold where *that* came from," says the miner. "Bags of it! Piles of it! Come along with me, pardner, and see the Elephant!"

Lorenzo and I are rarin' to go!

"Humph," says Papa. "Looks like fool's gold to me."

I peek over his shoulder and spell out a strange word on the map: "G-I-L-A
Trail. How do you say it, Papa?"

"Hee-la," he says. "It's the name of a river, they tell me."

But Mama doesn't like the new map at all.

"It goes from Nowhere through Nothing to No Place!" she cries.

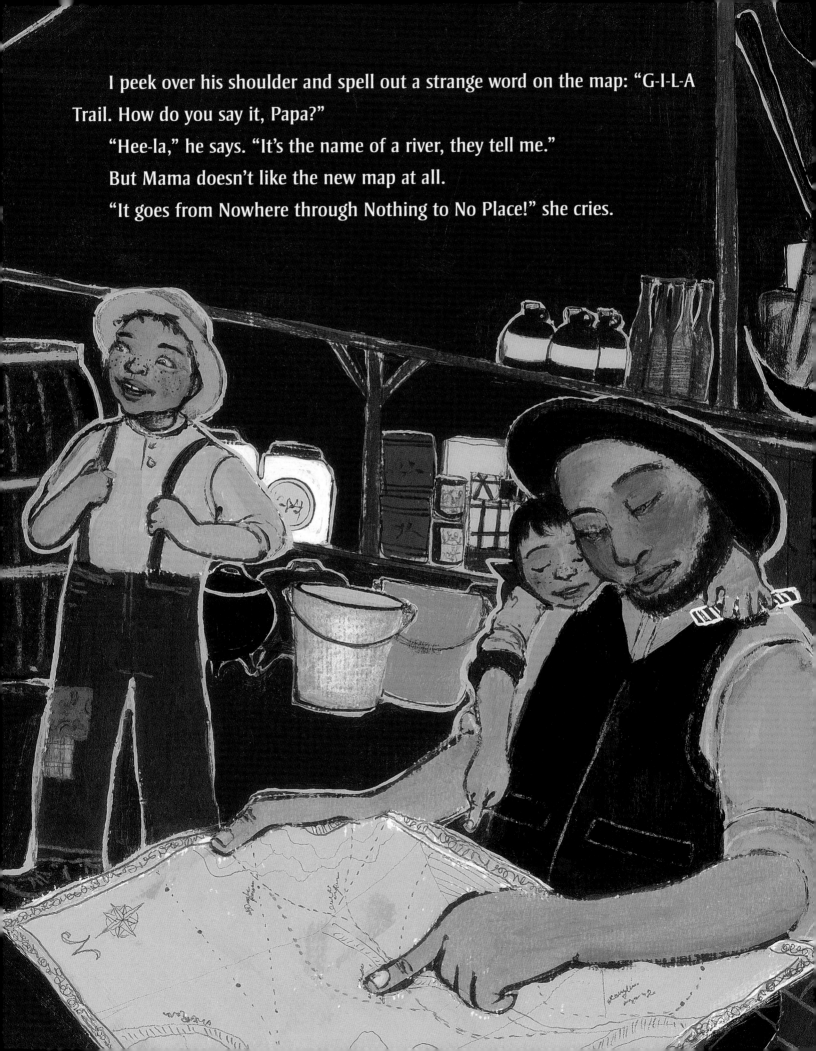

But way far away on the edge of the map is California! So off we go, slow as molasses, till late one afternoon, clouds puff up from little lambs to terrible rumbling herds of . . . elephants!

Boom! Doom! Here comes a flood! And Grandma runs lickety-split, just as fast as me.

Inside the wagon we all huddle together and hope we won't wash away.
Pretty soon, Grandma starts a-sewin' and Lorenzo starts to hum:

"It rained all night the day I left,
The weather was so dry.
The sun so hot I froze to death,
Susanna, don't you cry!"

Mile after long, long mile we go, stitch after tiny stitch.

Now we're a-drivin' down Doubtful Canyon, eight miles long and one wagon wide. Doubtful Canyon leads to Apache Pass.

Night comes—seems like the rocks split open—and ten men jump out!

They're sure-enough, out-and-out, genuine Apaches.

"Cochise," says the tallest one, pointing to himself. Then his hand shoots out . . . and rubs Papa's head. My papa's got no more hair than a boiled egg. And those Apaches laugh till they're fit to bust.

"Mercy!" gasps Mama. "They think you've already been scalped!"

Cochise gives a signal and—*whoosh!*—his men disappear, but he sets himself down beside us all nice and cozy for the night.

"Jiminy!" says Lorenzo. "We're going to wake up dead."

But Cochise points to himself again. *"Bueno,"* he says. "Good."

The campfire sinks down to ashes, and, far away, wolves howl. Stars poke through the night sky like millions of pins.

In the morning Cochise gives Papa a quiver made of mountain lion skin and filled with arrows, and Grandma gives Cochise a most beauteous piece of ruby-red silk, which he ties around his head. Then he folds his arms and waits and watches till the wagons roll away.

And so on and on we go, slow, slow, slow. The desert sun grows hotter
every day.

"Why don't the cactus trees have any leaves?" I want to know.
"Why's the sky so powerful big? Why don't we see the Elephant?"
They're all too tired to answer me.

But then we reach the Gila River, cool and green, where kind Pima people give us watermelon and sweet corn. They paint their faces with beautiful colors. My! Don't they look BO-dacious! Don't I wish *I* could!

And here a stranger joins our wagon train.

She's my baby sister, Gila, named for the river where she was born. She cries, but Mama smiles, and smiles, and smiles.

I sing the baby a lullaby:

"A buckwheat cake was in her mouth, A tear was in her eye. I said, 'I come from Dixieland.' Oh! Gila, don't you cry!'"

Then we follow Gila's river till it runs right into the big brown Colorado River. On the other side of the Colorado is . . . California.

"Listen, everybody!" I holler. *"Where's the Elephant?"*

"Hold your horses, Lily Rose," says Papa, shading his eyes. "Still a ways to go, I reckon."

And so there is. On the other side of the river lies the horriblest desert I ever did see. Sand hills. Sand storms. Sand fleas! And *this* trail is chock-full of *bones*. "Lorenzo," I whisper, "are they—ELEPHANT BONES?"

But just then, the poor tired oxen lift up their noses. Sniff, sniff. Do they smell water?

They do!

A year goes by, just like that. *Poof!*

Orange trees grow all around our new house. Little Baby Gila is *that* high, and Mr. Lorenzo has finally found himself a really-truly golden nugget that's almost as big as a pea.

And looky here! Many little needles fly quick, quick, quick. Our California friends have come to help us finally sew our quilt together, piece by piece and east to west.

"Every quilt tells a story," Grandma says. "You write it with a needle and you read it with your heart."

"Our whole trip is in that quilt," says Mama.

"What about the Elephant, Lily Rose?" Lorenzo teases. "Did you ever see it?"

And all at once I do. It's the whole long journey, step by step and stitch by stitch, and it's splendiferous. It's rumbustious. It's BO-dacious! Yes, I see the Elephant from trunk to tail. WHOOP-DE-DOO!

Do you?

WHOOP-DE-DOO!

Missouri
April 15, 1859

AUTHOR'S NOTE

Like quilters, writers often turn snippets of old things into something new. *The Elephant Quilt* is fiction, but it contains many colorful scraps of information gathered from books, letters, diaries, sketches, maps, family histories, photographs, songs, and objects. And it all began with a real girl and a real quilt.

Approximately one of every five travelers going west on the overland trails was a boy or a girl, and they left us some fascinating accounts of their adventures, including one very special visual journal created by young Mary Margaret Hezlep and her family. In 1859 the Hezleps traveled by wagon from Illinois to California. As they rolled along they recorded the tale of their trip in cloth, thread, and ink on the squares of a quilt, which now belongs to Mary Margaret's great-granddaughter. That quilt was the inspiration for this book.

In the 1800s, "to see the elephant" was a popular American expression, which meant to have the thrill, or shock, of a lifetime. Ventures into the unknown West were bound to lead to surprises—like the friendly meeting with the fierce Apache chief Cochise that a young girl named Sally Fox reported in her diary, also in 1859. Many grateful nineteenth-century visitors described both the generosity and the beautifully painted faces of the Pima (more correctly, Akimel O'othham) and the Maricopa (Xalychidom Piipaash). Their descendants still live near the Gila River in Arizona, where in 1851 a baby named Gila Thompson really was born.

My grandfather was born in Arizona, too, in 1896, and as a boy of ten he made an exciting wagon trip home from California with his father. Along the way they escaped from bandits in the desert and crossed the Colorado River in the midst of a great flood. When they finally got to Phoenix, a kindly storekeeper gave my grandfather a bag of jelly beans. My grandfather put the candy in the wagon and walked along behind it. Every so often a jelly bean jounced out of the bag, fell through a crack in the wagon floor, and tumbled into the sand. And one by one my grandfather ate them. This wonderful game—and the jelly beans— lasted almost all the way home to Tucson.

I loved to hear him tell stories like these, which bring the dim past nearly close enough to touch. When we piece them together, we see something just as warm and bright and BO-dacious as Lily Rose's Elephant Quilt.

SELECTED SOURCES
Of the several hundred primary and secondary sources I consulted, these were the most useful.

Laury, Jean Ray, and the California Heritage Quilt Project. *Ho for California! Pioneer Women and Their Quilts.* New York: E. P. Dutton, 1990.

Myres, Sandra L., ed. *Ho for California! Women's Overland Diaries from the Huntington Library.* San Marino, Calif.: Huntington Library, 1980.

Werner, Emmy E. *Pioneer Children on the Journey West.* Boulder, Colo.: Westview Press, 1995.

ESPECIALLY RECOMMENDED FOR YOUNG READERS

Erickson, Paul. *Daily Life in a Covered Wagon.* Preservation, 1995. New York: Puffin Books, 1997.

Paul, Ann Whitford. *Eight Hands Round: A Patchwork Alphabet.* New York: HarperCollins, 1991. Rpt. HarperTrophy, 1996.

Willing, Karen B., and Julie Bates Dock. *Quilting Now & Then.* Ashland, Ore.: Now & Then Publications, 1994.

To Mary, who saw the Elephant in the quilt
—S.L.
To Rob, Finn, and Emma with love
—S.D.M.

Text copyright © 2008 by Susan Lowell
Pictures copyright © 2008 by Stacey Dressen-McQueen
All rights reserved
Distributed in Canada by Douglas & McIntyre Ltd.
Color separations by Chroma Graphics PTE Ltd.
Printed and bound in China by South China Printing Co. Ltd.
Designed by Jay Colvin
First edition, 2008
1 3 5 7 9 10 8 6 4 2

www.fsgkidsbooks.com

Library of Congress Cataloging-in-Publication Data
Lowell, Susan, date.
    The elephant quilt : stitch by stitch to California / Susan Lowell ; pictures by Stacey
Dressen-McQueen.— 1st ed.
        p. cm.
    Summary: Lily Rose and Grandma stitch a quilt that tells the story of their
family's journey from Missouri to California by covered wagon in 1859.
      ISBN-13: 978-0-374-38223-0
      ISBN-10: 0-374-38223-9
    [1. Overland journeys to the Pacific—Fiction.   2. Quilting—Fiction.]   I. Dressen-
McQueen, Stacey, ill.   II. Title.

PZ7.L9648El 2008
[E]—dc22

                                                                        2005051227